Dear Ruby,
Always Be who you are
Never
change
Brooke ♡

Dear [Ruby,]
always be your
best self!
♡ madison

This book belongs to

Dear Ruby,
Always stay pretty
in your heart!
♡ Margot.

Mommy, am I pretty?

Margot L. Denommé © illustrated by Madison & Brooke Denommé-Warren

© 2013 by Margot L. Denommé

ISBN number : 978-0-9920340-0-9

Printed by Friesens in Canada

I would like to thank my editor Carol Watterson from Cubehouse Productions and graphic designer Alex Hennig of ClearDesign.

A portion of the proceeds from this book will be donated to Meagan's Walk: Creating a Circle of Hope. (www.meaganswalk.com)

www.mommyamiprettybook.com

Dedication

I thank my daughters, Madison and Brooke,
for the privilege of working with them on this book.
They fill my life with love and laughter.
I also thank my husband, Rob, for his support.

I wrote this book for all of the little girls
who struggle with the question, "Am I pretty?"

I dedicate this book to my mom and dad,
who taught me very early in life that
true beauty comes from within.

At school one day, Molly's best friend asked her if she looked pretty. Molly said "yes", but she wasn't sure what being pretty really meant.

Later, while walking home from school,
Molly asked her mother, "Mommy, am I pretty?"

"Do you feel pretty in your heart?" her mother asked.

Molly replied "Why? I just want to know
if you think I am pretty?"

"Do you know what being pretty means?"
her mother asked.

Molly shook her head, "no".

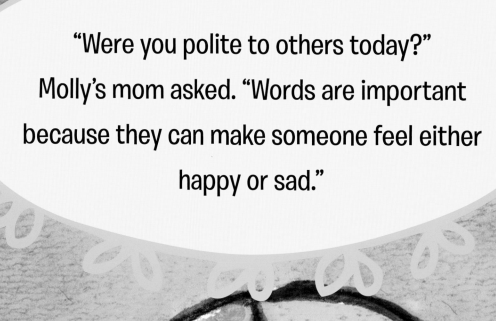

"Were you polite to others today?" Molly's mom asked. "Words are important because they can make someone feel either happy or sad."

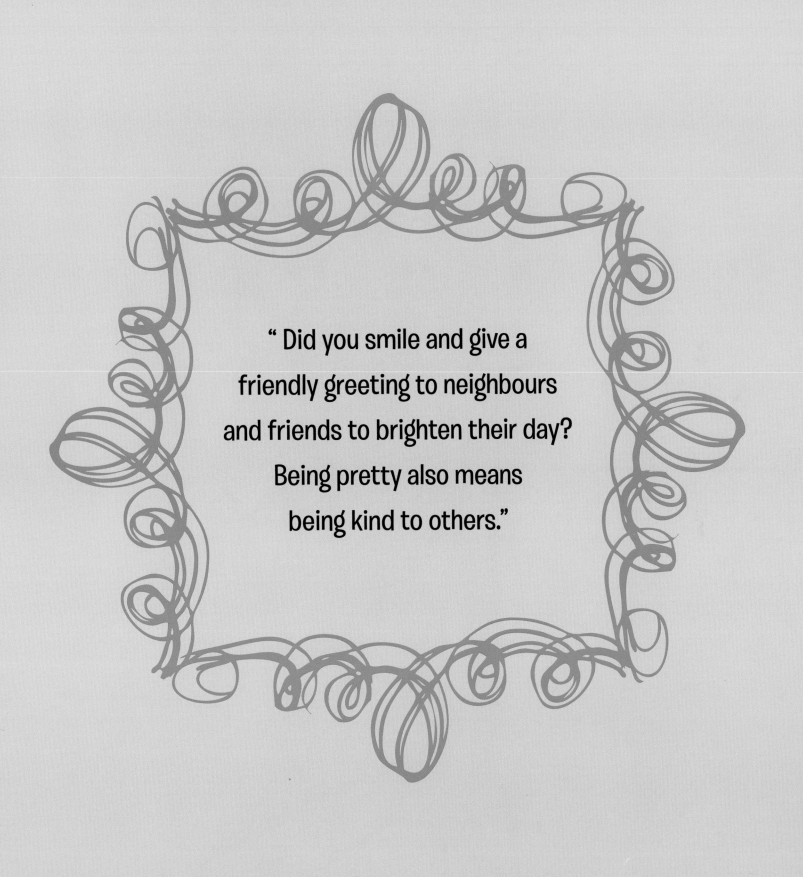

" Did you smile and give a
friendly greeting to neighbours
and friends to brighten their day?
Being pretty also means
being kind to others."

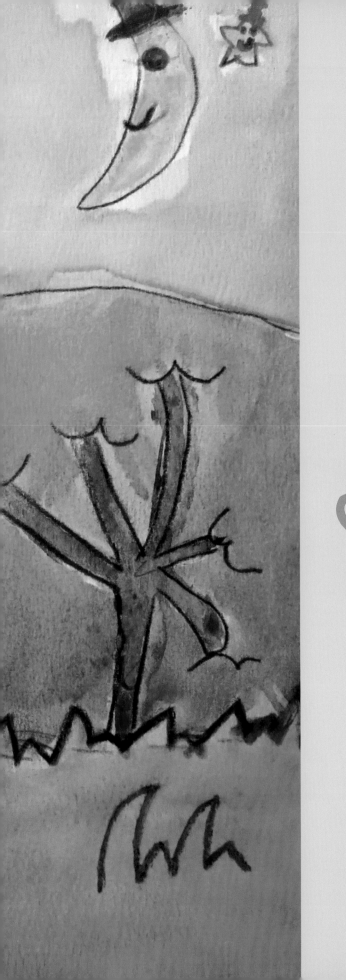

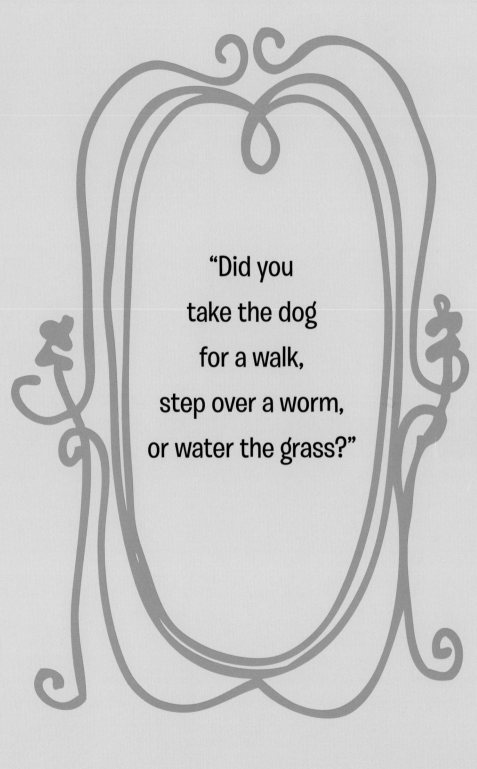

"Did you
take the dog
for a walk,
step over a worm,
or water the grass?"

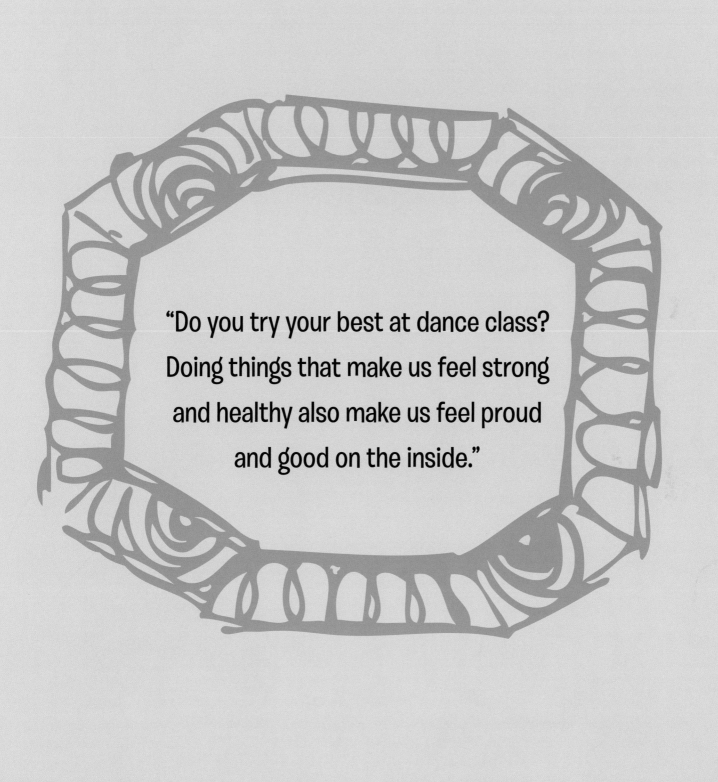

"Do you try your best at dance class? Doing things that make us feel strong and healthy also make us feel proud and good on the inside."

"Do you take the time to share
with your brother, sister, or a friend?

Together you can make beautiful music."

"Did you include the new girl
at school when you were playing
with your friends in the park?"
Molly's mother asked.

"Always try to include new friends
so they don't feel alone and left out.
It's important to treat others the
way you want them to treat you."

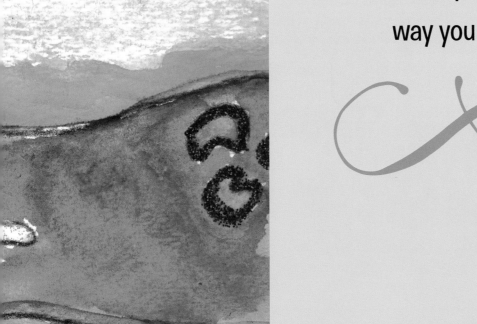

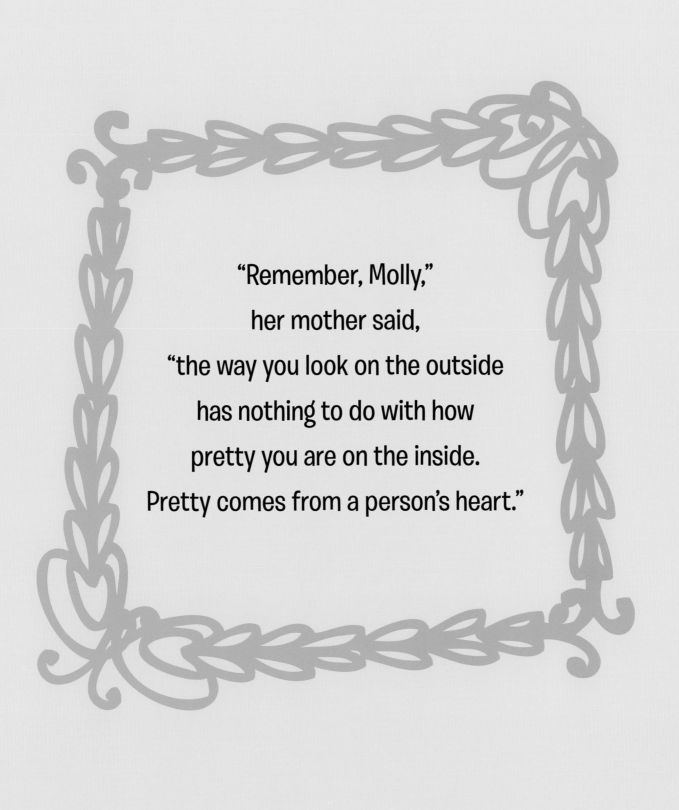

"Remember, Molly,"
her mother said,
"the way you look on the outside
has nothing to do with how
pretty you are on the inside.
Pretty comes from a person's heart."

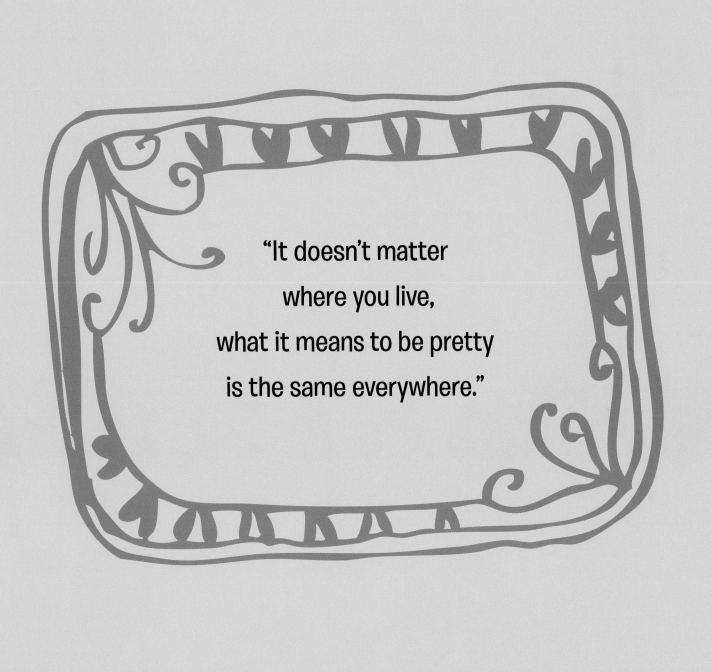

"It doesn't matter
where you live,
what it means to be pretty
is the same everywhere."

"Pretty is how you make the people around you feel. It's what's in YOUR heart that makes you pretty. It doesn't matter whether you are tall, short, big, or small. Always remember that when you walk into a room you can light it up with your smile."

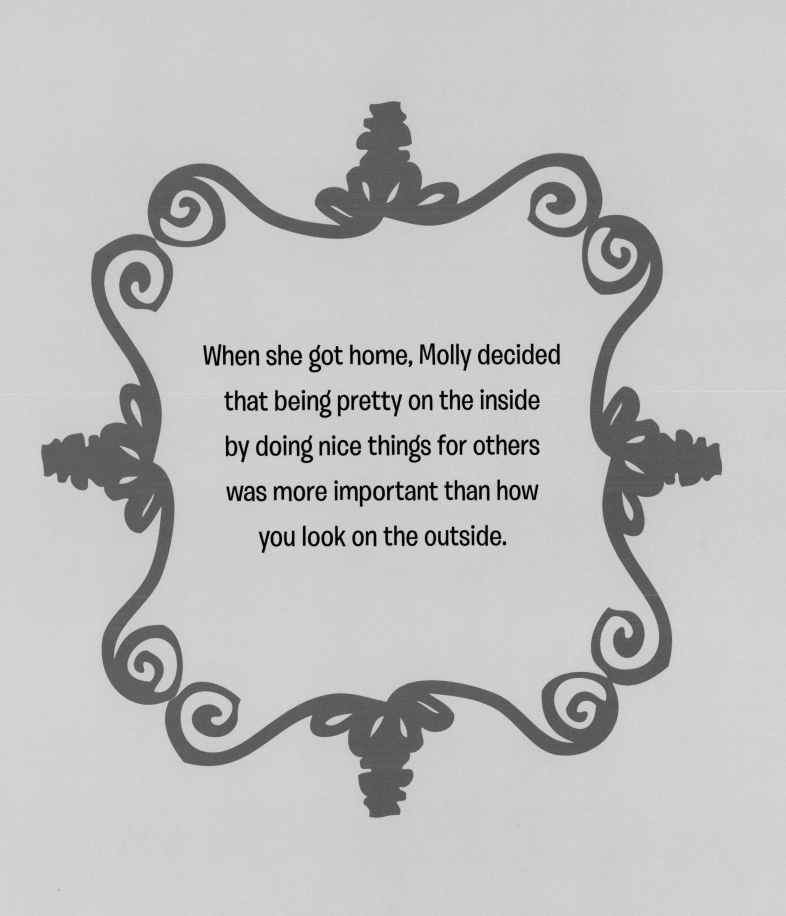

When she got home, Molly decided
that being pretty on the inside
by doing nice things for others
was more important than how
you look on the outside.

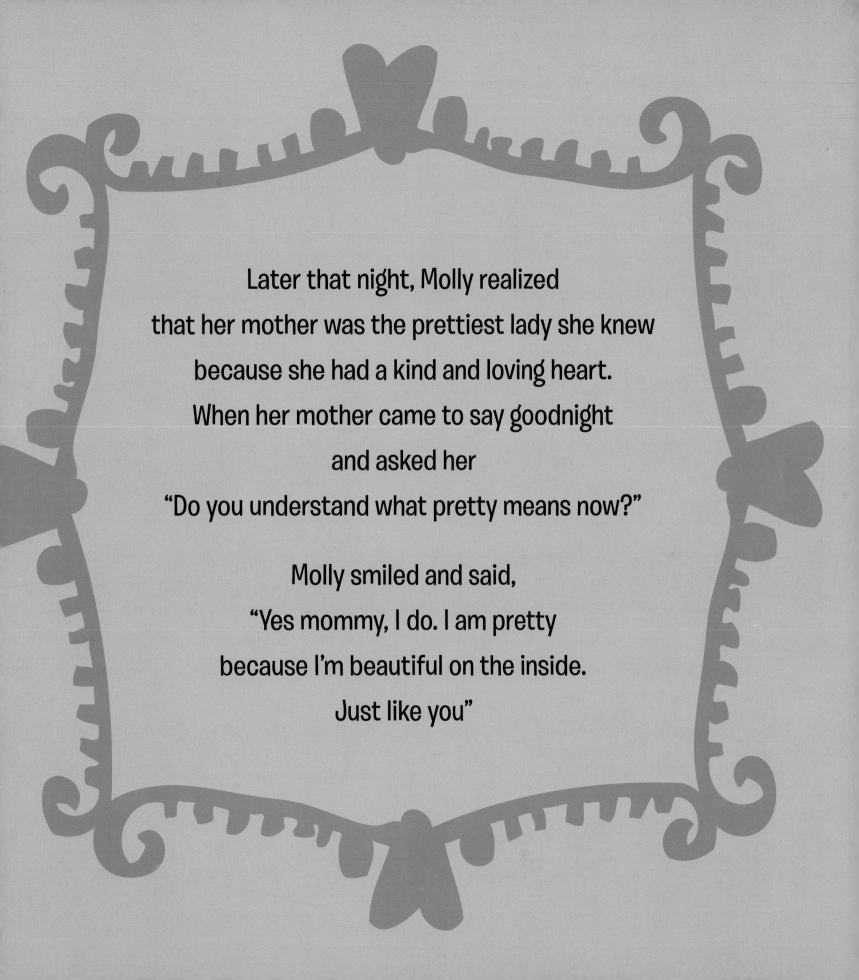

Later that night, Molly realized
that her mother was the prettiest lady she knew
because she had a kind and loving heart.
When her mother came to say goodnight
and asked her
"Do you understand what pretty means now?"

Molly smiled and said,
"Yes mommy, I do. I am pretty
because I'm beautiful on the inside.
Just like you"

The next day Molly couldn't wait
to go back to school to tell her best friend
that they were both pretty.

About the Author

Margot L. Denommé practices law in Toronto, Ontario where she lives with her husband Rob and two daughters. She wrote this book to encourage dialogue between parents, grandparents, caregivers, teachers, and young girls with a view to empower and teach them that true beauty lies within each and every one of them.

About the Illustrators

Both Madison and Brooke share a love of skiing, soccer and paddling. Madison, 11 years old, also enjoys track and field and volleyball. Brooke is 9 years old and loves acting and gymnastics. Art is a passion for both girls and they have created the illustrations for this book over the past 2 years.